I WANT to BE in a SCARY STORY

Sean Taylor

Jean Jullien

For dancing Rob – S.T.

For Lou – J.J.

WALKER BOOKS
AND SUBSIDIARIES
LONDON · BOSTON · SYDNEY · AUCKLAND

First published 2017 by Walker Books Ltd, 87 Vauxhall Walk, London SE11 5HJ · This edition published 2018 · Text © 2017 Sean Taylor · Illustrations © 2017 Jean Jullien · The right of Sean Taylor and Jean Jullien to be identified as author and illustrator respectively of this work has been asserted by them in accordance with the Copyright, Designs and Patents Act 1988 · This book has been typeset in URW Egyptienne T and Futura Bold · Printed in China · All rights reserved. No part of this book may be reproduced, transmitted or stored in an information retrieval system in any form or by any means, graphic, electronic or mechanical, including photocopying, taping and recording, without prior written permission from the publisher. · British Library Cataloguing in Publication Data: a catalogue record for this book is available from the British Library · ISBN 978-1-4063-8000-2 · www.walker.co.uk · 10 9 8 7 6 5 4 3 2 1

FSC
MIX
Paper from
responsible sources
www.fsc.org   FSC® C008047

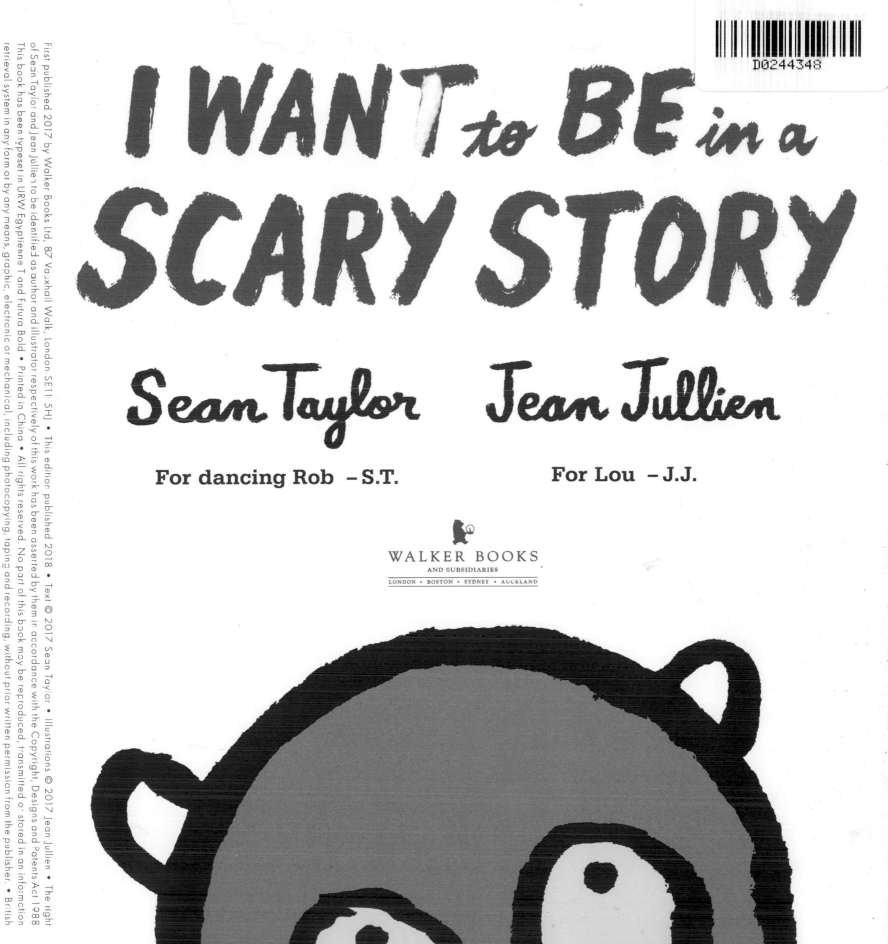

Hello, Little Monster.

What do you want to do today?

So, can I be in a story again tomorrow?

Now that WAS scary, Little Monster!

And that was FUNNY, too!

Little
Monster?
This isn't
funny!

The forest is dark and scary!

Are you
out here?

Little
Monster?

Monster! Are you OK?

Unless... what? Hey, Little

**Not for me
it won't be!**

It's not fair if his friend's **GINORMOUS** like that!

But you said you want this to be a **FUNNY** story now, didn't you?

Yes...

Well, it's going to be funny if a ginormous monkey and a teeny weeny monkey start chasing a monster, isn't it?

Good! That's going to be much funnier and better!

Who is going to be in there?

The witch.

WHAT?

Look, can't we maybe change
this book so it's a FUNNY story?!

All right, Little Monster.
There could be just a
teeny weeny monkey
and his friend
in there.

Wait a moment...

All right!

HOLD ON! This is too scary!

Well, you did say you wanted to be in a scary story.

I know. But...
I want to be in a scary story where *I* do the scaring!

Oh, *you* want to be the scary one?

YEAH!

OK then. You can creep up the stairs, sneak over to the door and then ...
SCARE THE PERSON INSIDE!

OK.
A ghost.

Would you rather
something else jumped out,
instead of the witch?

Maybe.

How about a ghost?

OK.

Is that *too* spooky?

A little bit.
But never mind.

Well, now something scary
is going to happen.

What?

You go inside,
and a creepy witch
will jump out.

That sounds better!

Is that too scary?

It MIGHT be.

Would you rather
it was just a
spooky house?

You bet I am!

All right. What sort of story?

I want to be in a **SCARY** story!

A *funny* story might be more fun.

Not for me it won't be!

OK. We could start the story in a dark and scary forest.

That's a good idea.

You ready then, Little Monster?

Can I be in a story?

I want to be in a SCARY story!